reasonable doubt

reasonable doubt

WHITNEY G.

This is a work of fiction. Names, characters, places, and incidents either are the product of the author's imagination or are used fictitiously, and any resemblance to actual persons, living or dead, business establishments, events, or locales is entirely coincidental.

Copyright © 2014 by Whitney G.

All rights reserved. No part of this book may be reproduced, stored in a retrieval system, or transmitted in any form, or by any means, electronic, mechanical, photocopying, recording or otherwise, without prior permission of the author.

Cover designed by Najla Qambers of Najla Qambers Designs
http://najlaqamberdesigns.com/

ISBN: 149910877X
ISBN 13: 9781499108774

For my BFF/ultimate beta-reader/amazing assistant/ shoulder to cry on whenever I'm acting crazy/ "person" like they say on 'Grey's Anatomy'... Tamisha Draper.

My books would suck without you...

table of contents

Prologue ix
Contract (n.): 1
Perjury (n.): 15
Burden of Proof (n.): 30
Conviction (n.): 40
Cross Examination (n.): 45
Recess (n.): 60

prologue

Andrew

New York City is nothing more than a shit-filled wasteland, a dump where failures are forced to drop all their broken dreams and leave them far behind. The flashing lights that shined brightly years ago have lost their luster, and that fresh feeling that once permeated the air—that *hopefulness*, is long gone.

Every person I once considered a friend is now an enemy, and the word "trust" has been ripped from my vocabulary. My name and reputation are tarnished thanks to the press, and after reading the headline that *The New York Times* ran this morning, I've decided that tonight will be the last night I ever spend here.

I can't deal with the cold sweats and nightmares that jerk me out of my sleep anymore, and as hard as I try to pretend like my heart hasn't been obliterated, I doubt that the agonizing ache in my chest will ever go away.

To properly say goodbye, I've ordered the best entrées from all my favorite restaurants, watched *Death of a Salesman* on Broadway, and smoked a Cuban cigar on the Brooklyn Bridge. I've also booked the penthouse suite at the Waldorf Astoria, where I'm now leaning back on the bed and threading my fingers through a woman's hair—groaning as she slides her mouth over my cock.

Teasingly darting her tongue around my tip, she whispers, "Do you like this?" as she looks up at me.

I don't answer. I push her head down and exhale as she presses her lips against my balls, as she covers my cock with her hands and moves them up and down.

Over the past two hours, I've fucked her against the wall, forced her to bend over a chair, and pinned her legs to the mattress while I devoured her pussy.

It's been quite fulfilling—*fun*, but I know this feeling will only last for so long; it never stays. In less than a week, I'll have to find someone else.

As she takes me deeper and deeper into her mouth, I tightly tug her hair—tensing as she bobs her head up and down. Pleasure begins to course its way through me, and the muscles in my legs stiffen—forcing me to let go and warn her to pull away.

She ignores me.

She grips my knees and sucks faster, letting my cock touch the back of her throat. I give her one last chance to move away, but since her lips remain wrapped around me, she leaves me no choice but to cum in her mouth.

And then she swallows.

Every. Last. Drop.

Impressive…

Finally pulling away, she licks her lips and leans back against the floor.

"That was my first time swallowing," she says. "I did that just for you."

"You shouldn't have." I stand and zip my pants. "You should've saved it for someone else."

"Right. Well, um…Do you want to order some dinner? Maybe we could eat it over HBO and go at it again afterwards?"

I raise my eyebrow, confused.

This is always the most annoying part, the part when the woman who previously agreed to "One dinner. One night. No repeats." wants to establish some type of imaginary connection. For whatever reason, she feels like there needs to be some type of closure conversation, some bland reassurance that'll confirm that what just happened was 'more than sex,' and we'll become friends.

But it *was* just sex, and I'm not in need of any friends. Not now, not ever.

"No, thank you." I walk over to the mirror on the other side of the room. "I have someplace to be."

"At three in the morning? I mean, if you just want to skip the HBO and go for another round instead, I can…"

I tune out her irritating voice and begin to button my shirt. I've never spent the night with a woman I met online, and she isn't going to be the first.

As I adjust my tie, I look down and spot a tattered pink wallet on the dresser. Picking it up, I flip it open and run my fingers across the name that's printed onto her license: Sarah Tate.

Even though I've only known this woman for a week, she's always answered to "Samantha." She's also told me—*repeatedly*, that she works as a nurse at Grace Hospital. Judging by the Wal-Mart employee card that's hiding behind her license, I'm assuming that part isn't true either.

I look over my shoulder, where she's now sprawled across the bed's silk sheets. Her creamy colored skin is unmarred and smooth; her bow shaped lips are slightly swollen and puffy.

Her green eyes meet mine and she slowly sits up, spreading her legs further apart, whispering, "You know you want to stay. *Stay…*"

My cock starts to harden—it's definitely up for another round, but seeing her real name has ruined any chance of that for me. I can't stand to be around anyone who's lied to me, even if she does have double D tits and a mouth from heaven.

I toss the wallet into her lap. "You told me your name was Samantha."

"Okay. *And*?"

"Your name is *Sarah*."

"So what?" She shrugs, beckoning me with her hand. "I never give my *real name* to men I meet on the internet."

"You just fuck them in five star hotel suites?"

"Why do you suddenly care about my real name?"

"*I don't.*" I glance at my watch. "Are you spending the night in this room or do I need to give you cab money to get home?"

"*What?*"

"Was my question unclear?"

"Wow…Just, wow…" She shakes her head. "How much longer do you think you'll be able to keep doing this?"

"Keep doing *what*?"

"Chatting someone up for a week, fucking her, and moving on to the next. How much longer?"

"Until my dick stops working." I put on my jacket. "Do you need cab fare or are you staying? Check out is at noon."

"Do you know that men like you—*relationship avoiders*, are the type that typically fall the hardest?"

"Did they teach you that at Wal-Mart?"

"Just because someone from your past hurt you doesn't mean that every woman after her will." She purses her lips. "That's probably why you are the way you are. Maybe if you tried to actually *date* someone you'd be a lot happier. You should take her out for dinner and actually listen, see her to her door without expecting an invitation inside, and maybe bypass the whole 'let's go fuck' in the hotel suite thing at the end."

Where are my keys? I need to go. Now.

"I can see it now…" She can't seem to shut up. "You're going to want more than sex one day, and the person you want it from is going to be someone you least expect. Someone who will force you to give in."

I pull my keys from underneath her crumpled dress and sigh. "Do you need cab money?"

"I have my own car, dick-face." She rolls her eyes. "Are you really this incapable of having a regular conversation? Would it kill you to talk to me for a few minutes after sex?"

"We have nothing more to discuss." I put my room key on the nightstand and walk toward the door. "It was very nice meeting you, Samantha, *Sarah*. Whatever the hell your name is. Have a great night."

"*Screw you!*"

"Three times was more than enough. No, thank you."

"Things are going to catch up to you one day, asshole!" She yells as I step into the hallway. "Karma is one hell of a bitch!"

"I know." I toss back. "I fucked her two weeks ago…"

contract (n.):

An agreement between two people that creates an obligation to do or not do a particular action.

Andrew

Six years later...
Durham, North Carolina

The woman who was currently sitting across from me was a fucking liar.

Dressed in an ugly ass grey sweater and a red plaid skirt, her hair looked as if it'd been dyed with a box of crayons. She looked nothing like the woman in the picture online, nothing like the smiling blonde with C-cup breasts, butterfly tattoos, and plump, pink lips.

Before I'd agreed to this date, I'd specifically asked for three separate proof of truth pictures: one of her holding a newspaper with the most recent date on it, one of her biting her lip, and one of her holding up a sign with her name on it. When I requested these things, she'd laughed and said that I was "the most paranoid person ever," but she'd done them. Or so I thought. With the exception of telling her my real name—I stopped giving out my real name years ago, I'd been completely honest and I expected that in return.

"Well, now that we're *alone*..." She suddenly smiled, revealing a mouth full of metal and rubber bands. "It's nice to finally meet you in person, *Thoreau*. How are you today?"

I didn't have time for this. "Who's the girl in your profile picture?" I asked.

"What?"

"*Who is the girl in your profile picture?*"

"Oh...Well, that isn't me."

"*No shit* it isn't you." I rolled my eyes. "Did you hire a model? Buy a bunch of stock images and use Photoshop?"

"Not exactly." She lowered her voice. "I just thought you'd be more likely to talk to me if I used that photo instead of my own."

I looked her over again, now noticing the strange unicorn tattoo across her knuckles and the "Love is blind" quote that was inked onto her wrist.

"What were you expecting to happen when we actually *met*?" This shit was boggling my mind. "Did you *think* about what would happen when that day came? When I realized that you weren't who you said you were?"

"I was kind of expecting for you to have lied about your picture too," she said. "I didn't know that you would really look like *you*, you know? This is the first time a guy on *Date-Match* has told the truth. I think it's a *sign*."

"*It's not.*" I shook my head. "And the model? How did you get someone to take all those pictures?"

"It wasn't a model. It was my roommate." Her eyes widened as I stood up. "Wait a second! All the things I said to you on the phone were absolutely true. I *am* interested in politics, and I do love studying the law and keeping up with high profile cases."

"What law school did you go to?"

"Law school?" She raised her eyebrow. "No, not *law school* type of law. Law like, I've watched every episode of *SVU* and I've read all of John Grisham's books."

I sighed and pulled a few bills out of my wallet, putting them on the table. I'd wasted enough time with her.

"Goodbye, *Charlotte*." I walked away, ignoring the rest of her apology.

The moment the valet pulled my car around, I slipped inside and sped off.

This shit is getting ridiculous...

This was the sixth time this had happened to me this month, and I didn't understand why someone would willingly lie with a potential face to face meeting on the line. It didn't make any fucking sense.

Annoyed, I picked up a bottle of scotch from the store across the street, and made a mental note to block this latest liar from my page. I was starting to feel like I'd run out of available women to sleep with in Durham. I was also starting to feel like I needed to switch cities and start all over again; the cold sweats from years ago had returned, and I knew the nightmares were coming next.

As soon as I stepped into my condo, I poured myself three shots and tossed them back. Then I poured three more.

I scrolled through my phone and checked my emails for the day—client referrals, more requests to chat from *Date-Match*, and a message from the sexy blonde I was supposed to meet this Saturday.

The subject-line read, "Honesty is Key, right?"

I tossed back another shot before opening it, hoping it was an invitation to meet tonight instead.

It wasn't. It was a goddamn essay.

"Hey, Thoreau. I know we're supposed to meet each other this Saturday and trust me, I was sooo looking forward to it, but I need to know that you're interested in me for me and not my looks. I've met a lot of creepy guys on here because they just like my picture, and when we meet, they just want to have sex. I can assure you that I am who I say I am, but I'm looking for something a little more

fulfilling than casual sex. We don't have to have a full blown relationship, or engage in an intense affair, but we could at least build a friendship first, you know? I'm looking forward to seeing you, so let me know if you're still interested in meeting me—Liz."

I immediately clicked on my profile and opened the "What I'm Looking For" box, making sure that it still read the same: "Casual sex. Nothing more. Nothing Less."

That line wasn't there for decoration, and it was in bold print for a reason.

I returned to the woman's message and responded. *"I am no longer interested in meeting you. Best of luck finding whatever you're looking for –Thoreau."*

"Are you for real?" She replied instantly. *"You can't use another friend? We can't be 'just friends'?—Liz."*

"Hell no—Thoreau." I signed off and blocked her address.

Another shot made its way down my throat, and I scrolled through the remaining emails—immediately opening the one that came from the only person I considered a friend in this city. Alyssa.

Subject: Desert Dick
So, I'm emailing you right now because I just thought about how much pain you're in currently…We haven't talked about you getting laid in quite a while, and that concerns me. Greatly. Like, I've CRIED about your lack of pussy…I'm very sorry that so many women have sent you fraudulent pictures and given you a severe case of blue balls. I'm attaching the links to a top of the line lotion that I think you should invest in for the weeks to come.
Your dick is in my prayers,
—Alyssa.

I smiled and typed a response.

Subject: Re: Desert Dick

Thank you for your concerns about my dick. Although, seeing as though you've NEVER discussed getting laid, I think having Cobweb Pussy is a far more serious illness. Yes, it is true that so many women have sent me pictures, but it's quite sad that you've never sent me yours, isn't it? I'm more than willing to send you mine, and eventually help you cure your sad and unfortunate disease.

Thank you for telling me that my dick is in your prayers.
I'd prefer if it was in your mouth.
—Thoreau.

Just like that, my night was now ten times better. Even though I'd never met Alyssa in person and our conversations were restricted to phone calls, emails, and text messages, I felt a strong connection to her.

We'd met through an anonymous and exclusive social network—LawyerChat. There were no profile pictures, no newsfeed activity, only message boards. There was a small profile box where information could be placed (first name only, age, number of years practiced, high or low profile status), and a logo on each user's profile that revealed his or her sex.

Every user was "guaranteed" to be a lawyer who'd been personally invited via email. According to the site's developers, they'd "cross-referenced every practicing lawyer in the state of North Carolina against the board's licensing records to ensure a unique and one of a kind support system."

I honestly thought the network was bullshit, and if it weren't for the fact that I'd fucked a few of the women I'd met on there, I would've cancelled my account after the first month.

Nonetheless, when I saw a new "Need Some Advice" message from an "Alyssa," I couldn't resist trying to replicate my previous results. I read through her profile first—twenty seven, one year out of law school, book lover—and decided to go for it.

My intent was to answer her legal questions, slowly steer the conversation to more personal things, and then ask her to join *Date-Match* so I could see what she looked like. But she wasn't like the other women.

She sent me constant messages, and she always kept the topic of conversation professional. Since she was such a young and inexperienced lawyer, she asked for advice on the simplest topics: legal brief editing, claim filing, and exhibition of evidence. After we'd chatted five times and I'd grown tired of having three hour long info-dump sessions, I asked for her phone number.

She said no.

"Why not?" I'd typed.

"Because it's against the rules."

"I've never met a lawyer that hasn't broken at least one."

"Then you're not a very good lawyer. I'll find someone else to chat with now. Thanks."

"You're going to lose that case tomorrow." I typed before she could end our session. "You have no idea what you're doing."

"Are you really that upset about me not giving you my phone number? What are you, twelve?"

"Thirty two, and I don't give a fuck about your phone number. I was only asking for it so I could call and tell you that the brief you sent me is littered with typos, and the closing argument reads like a first year law student wrote it. There are too many mistakes for me to sit here and type them all."

"My brief isn't that bad."

"It's not that good either." Before I could sign out of our chat, her phone number appeared on the screen, and underneath it was a short paragraph: "If you're going to call and help me, fine. If you're using my number to talk me into joining a dating site later, then forget it. I joined this network for career support, that's it."

REASONABLE DOUBT

I stared at her message long and hard—debating whether I should help her with no chance of getting anything out of it, but something made me call her anyway. I walked her through every mistake she'd made, insisted that she clear up a few sentences, and even re-formatted her brief.

Just when I was about to tell her goodbye and hang up, the strangest thing happened. She asked, "How was your day today?"

"That's not in your brief." I said. "You only want to talk about lawyer shit, remember?"

"I can't change my mind?"

"No. Hang up." I waited to hear a beep, but the only thing I heard was laughter. If it wasn't for the fact that it was such a raspy and sexy sound, I would've hung up myself, but I couldn't put the phone down.

"I'm sorry," she said, still laughing. "I didn't mean to offend you."

"You didn't. Hang up."

"I don't want to." She finally stopped laughing. "I apologize for that hostile message I sent you…You're actually the only guy I've met on here who answers all my questions. Are you busy right now? Can you talk?"

"About *what*?"

"About yourself, your life…I've been asking you boring legal questions every day, and you've been very patient so…It's only fair that we talk about something less boring for once if we're going to be friends, right?"

Friends?

I was hesitant to respond—especially since it didn't seem like the 'less boring' topics would involve sex, and she'd said the word "friends" so easily. Yet, I was in the middle of another sex-less night already, so I began to have a regular conversation with her. Until five in the morning, she and I discussed the most mundane things—our daily lives, favorite books, her dream of becoming a late, professional ballerina.

A few days later, we spoke again, and after a month, I was talking to her every other day.

Tossing back another shot, I pressed the call button on my phone and waited to hear her soft voice.

No answer. I considered sending her a text, but then I realized it was nine o' clock on a Wednesday and we wouldn't be able to talk at all tonight.

Practice…Wednesday nights are always ballet practice…

———

"Mr. Hamilton?" My secretary stepped into my office the next morning.

"Yes, Jessica?"

"Mr. Greenwood and Mr. Bach would like to know if you want to participate in the next round of intern interviews today."

"*I don't.*"

"Okay…" She looked down and scribbled something onto her notepad. "Did you at least look over the resumes then? They have to narrow it down to fifteen today."

I sighed and pulled out the stack of resumes she'd given me last week. I'd read through them all and written notes, mostly— "Pass" "Double Pass" and "I don't feel like reading this." All the remaining applicants were from Duke University, and to my knowledge, we were the only firm in the city who accepted pre-law *and* law school applicants for paid internships.

"I wasn't impressed with any of the applicants." I slid the papers across my desk. "Was that the entire selection pool?"

"No, sir." She walked over and placed an even larger stack in front of me. "*This* is the entire selection pool. Do you need me to do anything else for you this morning?"

"Besides getting my coffee?" I pointed to the empty mug at the edge of my desk. I hated that I always had to remind her to bring it; I couldn't function in the morning without a fresh cup.

"I'm so sorry. I'll get that right away."

I turned on my computer and scrolled through my emails, sorting them all by importance. Of course, Alyssa's latest email was pushed straight to the top.

Subject: Get Over Yourself.

Thank you for the childish picture text of the white dust that was outside your condo this morning. I really appreciated it, but I can assure you that that is NOT what the inside of my vagina looks like right now.

Not that it's any of your business, but I don't need to get laid every other day to satisfy my needs. They are WELL taken care of with a VARIETY of tools.

—Alyssa

Subject: Re: Get Over Yourself.

I sent you *two* pictures. One of the white dust and one of a dried up lake with dying animals. Was the second picture more accurate?

The only tool your pussy needs is my tongue. It's here whenever you want it, and it works in a "VARIETY" of ways.

—Thoreau

"Here you are, Mr. Hamilton." Jessica suddenly set my coffee on the desk. "Can I ask you something?"

"No, you may not."

"I thought so," she said, lowering her voice and looking into my eyes. "I know this is a bit unprofessional, but I need a date for the gala next month."

"Then *find a date* for the gala next month."

"That was my way of asking *you* to be my date…"

I blinked. I needed to find a way to word this "Hell no" very carefully.

Jessica was fresh out of college—way too damn young for me, working here because her grandfather started this firm, and looking for much more than I'd ever be willing to give. I'd overheard her several times on her lunch breaks, talking about how she wanted to be married before she turned twenty five. She also apparently wanted to be a stay-at-home mom with six kids, and live in a house in the suburbs.

In other words, she was completely out of her fucking mind.

"So, what do you say?" She smiled.

I tried not to roll my eyes. "Jessica…"

"*Yes?*" Her eyes were full of hope.

"Look, sweetheart. Not only would it be highly inappropriate for the two of us to *ever* engage in any type of relationship outside of this office, but I'm not the man you're looking for. At all. Trust me."

"Not even for *one night?*"

"The words 'one night' in my book hold certain expectations that you couldn't possibly meet. So, *no*. Go do some work."

"Is 'one night' a code for sex?"

"Why are you still in my office?"

"I wouldn't tell anyone if we had sex," she whispered. "I've actually fantasized about it since we first met. And, since you never have any calls on the books from a girlfriend, I'm assuming you're available."

"*I'm not.*"

"I walked in on you while you were in the restroom once… You're at least nine inches I think."

What the fuck?!

I was five seconds away from recording this conversation on my phone and emailing it to her grandfather.

"I'm *really good* at giving blowjobs," she said. "I've been doing it since high school. All the guys I've blown have said my mouth is *amazing.*" She bit her lip.

"Is there super-glue on my floor? Is that why you're still standing there?"

"If you were my date to the gala and we ended up having a good time, you'd be the first man I'd actually went all the way with." She blurted out, blushing. "I'm still a virgin, *down there*."

"Then I'm *definitely* not the man for you." I rolled my eyes. "Now, leave before I call Mr. Greenwood and tell him that his precious granddaughter is offering to suck my dick over morning coffee."

Shocked, her cheeks tinged red and she quickly walked to the door. Then she looked over her shoulder and winked at me—fucking *winked* at me, before stepping out.

I immediately typed a note into my planner: *Find a new secretary—an older, married one...*

Before I could finish organizing my inbox, my cell phone rang. Alyssa.

"I'm busy," I answered.

"Then why did you pick up the phone?"

"Because the sound of my voice makes you wet."

"Funny." She laughed. "How's your morning?"

"Typical. My secretary just came onto me for the third time this month."

"She sent you another 'You and me belong together' note with chocolates?"

"No, she offered to suck my dick."

"What?" She gasped. "You're kidding!"

"Unfortunately not. After that, she told me she was willing to give me her virginity. Needless to say, I'll be posting a replacement ad pretty soon. Anyone from your office want to work for a better firm? I'll double the salary."

"How do you know that *my* firm isn't better than yours?"

"Because you call and ask me for advice on cases all the time—silly cases at that. If your firm was better, you'd never have to ask."

"Whatever." She groaned. "Have you bucked off the online dating wagon yet?"

"*Bucked? Wagon?*" I could never understand her little Southern metaphors. "What the hell does that mean?"

"Ugh, god..." She sighed. "It means you didn't update me about your date last night so I guess it was a bust, which means you haven't slept with anyone in over a month. That has to be a record for you."

"It is."

"Do you want some advice?"

"Not unless you want to come to my office and tell me *in person*." I smiled.

"No, thanks. Speaking of advice, I'll need your help Friday night."

"With what?"

"I just landed a pretty big case. I haven't gone through all the documents yet, but I already know I'm in over my head."

I leaned back in my chair. "If it's that big of a case, you could bring the documents to my condo tonight. I'd be happy to help you sort through them. Categorization has always been my specialty."

"Ha! Nice try, but I don't think so." She continued to talk about her case, but I was only halfway listening. It still struck me as odd that she didn't want to meet me in person, that she shut down the very thought any time I brought it up.

"Also..." She was still rambling. "I'll probably have to do some research on those changes. I'm not sure if—"

"Tell me the real reason why I can't meet you in person." I cut her off.

"*What?*"

"We've known each other for six months now. Why don't you want to meet?"

Silence.

"Do I need to repeat the question?" I stood up and walked over to my door, locking it. "Did you not understand me?"

"It's against the LawyerChat rules…"

"Fuck *LawyerChat*." I rolled my eyes. "It's against the rules for you and me to have each other's phone numbers in the first place, for us to act like fucking teenagers and make each other cum over the phone at night, but you've never complained about that."

"You've never made me cum…"

"Don't lie to me."

"You haven't."

"So, last week when I said that I wanted you to ride my mouth so I could eat your pussy until you came all over my lips, you were *pretending* to breathe hard?"

She sucked in a breath. "No, but—"

"I thought so. Why can't we meet in person?"

"Because it would ruin our friendship and you know it."

"*I don't.*"

"You've told me that you never sleep with the same woman twice, that after you sleep with someone you're done with her."

"I've never fucked one of my *friends* before."

"That's because I'm your only one."

"I'm aware, but—" I stopped. I had no defense for that.

Silence lingered over the line, and I tried to think of another argument.

She spoke up first. "I honestly don't want to ruin our friendship over one senseless fuck."

"I guarantee we'll have more than *one* senseless fuck."

Her light, airy laugh drifted over the line, and I sighed—attempting to envision what she looked like. I wasn't sure why, but over the past few weeks, I'd been longing to experience her laughter face to face.

"You know," she went on, "for a high profile lawyer, you have a pretty dirty mouth."

"You'd be surprised how much filthier it can get."

"Filthier than what I've already experienced?"

"*Much filthier.*" I'd been treading the waters since we began this friendship—still hopeful that we'd meet in person someday, but now that we weren't, there was no point in holding back. "I guess I'll *talk to you* tonight."

"Not unless you find another date between now and then. I know you'll be searching."

"Of course I'll be searching." I scoffed. "Is Alyssa your *real* name?"

"Yes, but I'm sure *Thoreau* isn't yours. Do you care to finally give it to me?"

"I'll give it to you when you come to your fucking senses and let me see you."

"You just won't let that go, will you?" She laughed again. "What if the real reason I don't want to meet you is because I'm ugly?"

"I have a good feeling that *you're not.*"

"But if I *was*?"

"I'd fuck you with the lights off."

"I prefer the lights *on.*"

"Then I'd make you wear a paper bag over your head."

"*WHAT?!*" She burst into giggles. "You're ridiculous! Ugh, there's a client at my door right now. I have to go. Can I call you later?"

"Always." I hung up, smiling. Then it hit me.

Fuck...She always finds a way out of that line of questioning...

perjury (n.):

The willful giving of false testimony under oath.

Alyssa (Well, my real name is "Aubrey"...)

"Lies always catch up to people in the end. Why don't people understand that?" That's what Thoreau's text message said this morning.

"You don't think some lies are justifiable?" I texted back.

"No. Never."

I hesitated. "So, you've never lied to me?"

"Why would I?"

"Because we barely know each other..."

"Only because you keep me at a distance." He sent me another text before I could respond. "Would you like to know my real name and where I work?"

"I prefer our anonymous arrangement."

"Of course you do, and I've never lied to you. I trust you for some strange reason."

"Some strange reason?"

"Very strange. I'll talk to you later."

I tossed my phone into my purse and sighed, letting that familiar feeling of guilt wash over me. I'd never meant to continue talking to him, to become his friend outside of LawyerChat, but I was in too deep, and I didn't want to let him go.

Months ago, when I'd spotted the invitation to the exclusive network on my mother's desk, I swore to only use it when I needed to ask questions for my pre-law classes. I'd used her access code to log in, built a fake profile, and made sure all the questions I asked were weaved in a way that no one would know that they were for homework assignments.

Unfortunately for me, the pre-law program at Duke was unlike any other program in the country. It consisted of more hands-on classes, one-on-one mentoring from practicing lawyers, and it was mandated that each student find an internship for the final four semesters. In addition to that, they expected us to read through and interpret case files like we were already lawyers.

If I had known that asking Thoreau for so much homework advice would lead to an actual friendship, I might have stopped talking to him sooner. Then again, just like I was his only friend, he was my only friend, too.

He was open and honest every time we spoke, and I only wished that I could be the same—especially since he seemed to have a habit of saying, "I hate fucking liars" whenever one of his dates deceived him.

Damnit...

Smoothing the tulle fabric of my tutu, I took several deep breaths; I could think about my friendship with Thoreau later, right now I needed to focus.

Today was audition day for a production of *Swan Lake* and I was a nervous wreck; I'd barely slept the night before, skipped breakfast, and showed up to the theater five hours early.

"Please clear the stage, ladies and gentlemen!" The director shouted from below. "The official auditions will begin in thirty minutes! Please clear the stage and make your way to the wings!"

Before heading backstage, I looked out into the audience. Most of the faces were familiar—my classmates, instructors, a few directors from the ballet company I'd worked for last summer, but the faces I needed to see weren't there.

They never were.

Hurt, I found a corner in the dressing room and called my mother.

"Hello?" she answered on the first ring.

"Why aren't you here?"

"Why aren't I *where*, Aubrey? What are you talking about *now*?" She let out an exasperated sigh.

"My open audition for *Swan Lake*. You promised that you and dad were coming."

"It's Aubrey, honey!" She yelled to my dad in the background. "Your recital was today?"

"I haven't been in a *recital* since I was thirteen." I gritted my teeth. "This is an audition, a once in a lifetime audition, and you're supposed to be here."

"I guess my secretary forgot to tell me about it this morning," she said. "Have you landed any internships for your major yet?"

"I have *two* majors."

"*Pre-law*, Aubrey."

"No." I sighed.

"Well, why not? Do you think one is just going to fall from the sky and land in your lap? Is that it?"

"I had an interview yesterday at Blaine and Associates," I said, feeling my heart grow heavier by the second, "and I have another one next week at Greenwood, Bach, and Hamilton. I'm also about to audition for the role of a lifetime if you'd like to pretend to give a fuck for five seconds."

"*Excuse me*, young lady?"

"You're not here." There were tears in my eyes. "*You're not here*...Do you know how huge this production is going to be?"

"Are you getting *paid*? Is the New York Ballet Company running it?"

"That's not the point. I've told you over and over how important this audition is to me. I called and reminded you last night, and it would be really nice if my *parents* showed up and believed in me for a change."

"Aubrey..." She sighed. "I do believe in you. I always have, but I'm in the middle of a huge hearing right now and you know that because it's all over the papers. You also know that becoming a professional ballerina is not a stable career choice, and as much as I would *love* to leave my high-paying client to watch you tiptoe around on stage—"

"It's called dancing *en pointe*."

"Same thing," she said. "Regardless, it's just an audition. I'm sure your father and I won't be the only parents who couldn't make it today. Once you graduate from college and get into law school, you'll see ballet for what it really is—*a hobby*, and you'll be grateful that we pushed you into double majoring."

"Ballet is my *dream*, mother."

"It's a phase, and you're way past the prime age for becoming a professional last time I checked. Remember how you suddenly up and quit at sixteen? You'll quit again, and it'll be for the best. As a matter of fact—"

I hung up.

I didn't want to listen to another one of her dream-killing speeches, and it angered me that she'd called ballet a "phase" when I'd been dancing since I was six years old. When she and my dad had poured countless dollars into private classes, costumes, and competitions.

The only reason why I'd "quit" at sixteen was because I'd broken my foot and couldn't audition for any of the dance schools anymore. And the only reason I started to show the faintest interest in law was because I couldn't do much outside of my rehab sessions except *read*.

My heart had always belonged in pointe slippers, and that fact would never change.

"Aubrey Everhart?" A man suddenly called my name from the theater door. "Is that you?"

"Yes."

"You're next to take the stage. Got about five minutes."

"Be right there..." I stuffed my bag into a locker. Before I could close it, my phone rang.

Knowing it was my mother calling to offer a half-assed apology, I tried my best not to scream. "Please spare me your apologies." I immediately picked up. "They don't mean anything to me anymore."

"I was calling to tell you good luck," a deep voice said.

"Two minutes!" A stagehand glared at me and motioned for me to head onto the stage.

"*Thoreau?*" I turned my back to the stagehand. "What are you telling me good luck for?"

"You mentioned having some type of audition weeks ago. It's today, right?"

"Yes, thank you..."

"You don't sound too excited about your *dream* right now."

"How can I be when my own parents don't believe in it?"

"You're *twenty seven years old.*" He scoffed. "Fuck your parents."

I laughed, guiltily. "I wish it was that simple..."

"It really is. You make your own money, and despite the fact that you don't really know shit about the law, you seem to be a pretty decent lawyer. Fuck them."

"I'll keep that in mind," I said, trying to steer that subject away. "I'm shocked you remembered that my audition was today."

"*I didn't.*" He hung up, and I knew he was smiling as he did that.

"Fifteen seconds, Miss Everhart!" The stagehand grabbed my arm and practically pulled me onto the stage.

I smiled at the judges and stood in fifth position—arms over my head, and waited for the first note of Tchaikovsky's composition to play.

There was a rustling of papers, a few coughs from someone in the audience, and then the music began.

I was supposed to demonstrate an arabesque, a pirouette, and then perform the routine that I'd been rehearsing in class for the past month and a half. I didn't feel like it, though, and since this was one of my last opportunities to make an impression, I decided to dance how I wanted.

I shut my eyes and completed pirouette after pirouette, fouette turn after fouette turn. I wasn't even on beat with the music, and I could tell the pianist was confused and trying to keep up with me.

I demonstrated every jump I knew, perfectly landing each one of them, and when the pianist gave up and struck the last note, I returned to fifth position—smiling.

There was no applause, no cheers, nothing. I tried to read the judges' faces to see if they looked mildly impressed, but they were stoic.

"That will be all, Miss Everhart," one of them said. "Will Miss Leighton Reynolds please take the stage?"

I murmured "Thank you" before stepping off and rushing out of the theater. I didn't bother watching the rest of the auditions.

For the remainder of the afternoon, I walked around campus and tried not to cry. When I was sure that no tears would fall, I sent emails to Thoreau; that was the only thing that could possibly make me feel better.

Subject: Thinking…
"One dinner. One night. No repeats." Do you pick a cheap or expensive restaurant? Do you pay for the dinner and the hotel room? Or do you make the woman split it with you?
—**Alyssa.**

Subject: Re: Thinking...
Expensive dinner. Five star hotel suite. I pay for everything. Would you like me to book a few reservations for us so I can show you?
—Thoreau.

Subject: Re: Re: Thinking...
Of course not. And a "few" reservations? What happened to just one?

Subject: Re: Re: Re: Thinking...
I told you I'd make an exception in your case. I invested in a box of paper bags today.
—Thoreau

I laughed and looked at my watch. It was five o' clock and I was sure the results for the production had been posted hours ago, but I was too scared to look. All I wanted was a chance to be a member of the swan corps, or even an understudy for the lead.

Why did I fuck up that routine? What the hell was I thinking?

After driving myself crazy with questions, I forced myself to make the trek back to the dance theater to look at the final cast posting. When I arrived, there was a huge crowd in front of the sign, and I could hear the usual "I'm in! I'm in!" and "How could they not pick me?" revelations.

I squeezed my way through everyone and squinted at the sheet, looking for my name on the minor cast sheet but it wasn't there.

It was on the *major* cast sheet, and right next to the lead role of Odette/Odile, the white and black swan, was my full name in bold.

I burst into tears, jumping up and down in disbelief. I wanted to call my mom and tell her the good news, but my heart suddenly sank at the thought.

I knew that at this very moment, she was probably telling my father that I'd hung up in her face, and that he needed to make sure I knew the strings behind them paying for my education: "If you drop pre-law, we'll stop writing the checks...Pre-law pays for your classes, ballet doesn't."

———

I lifted my aching feet out of a bucket of ice and patted them dry with a towel. I wasn't sure how I was going to juggle a leading role, classes, and a potential internship, but I didn't have a choice.

Sighing, I glanced at the calendar on my desk where I'd scribbled "Interview prep day" in today's slot.

My upcoming interview with Greenwood, Bach, and Hamilton—one of the most prestigious firms in the state, was more than just an interview. It was a *process*, and every intern-seeking student knew that landing an internship at that firm could do wonders for a resume.

The firm was so selective that they conducted four rounds of phone interviews, three online tests, and required each applicant to complete several essays before the final interview with the partners.

I'd soared through the phone interviews and the exams, but the essays—regarding hundred paged case files, were something that I hadn't expected. I'd even thought they'd sent me the wrong packet so I called to say, "I believe my packet was switched with the *law-school level* intern application." The secretary simply laughed at me.

She'd said the firm expected all of its interns—law school level *and* undergraduate level, to fill out the same packet to the best of their ability.

"Don't worry," she'd said. "We're not expecting perfection from you. We just want to see how your mind works."

I grabbed the case file that was giving me the most trouble and placed it into my lap. Then I went to the GBH firm's website and familiarized myself with the three partners who would be interviewing me.

Greenwood, the founder of the firm, was a salt and pepper haired man with wiry framed glasses. He touted Harvard as his reason for being so demanding and thorough, and boasted that in his thirty years of practicing the law, he'd attained one of the highest victory rates in the country.

Bach, partner of the firm for over ten years, was a bald man in his early forties, though he looked a bit older. He'd worked his way up through the firm, and since he was "such a hardworking individual with unparalleled passion," Greenwood had no choice but to make him his first partner. He had one of the second highest victory rates in the country.

Last was Hamilton—Andrew Hamilton, and he was…He was *sexy as fuck*. I tried to focus on his biography and ignore his picture, but I couldn't help it. His deep and piercing blue eyes were staring right at me, and his short, dark brown hair was begging my hands to run through it.

He had the face of a Greek God—evenly tanned, perfectly symmetrical, strong and chiseled jawline, and his full lips were curved into a slight smirk.

Even though the picture only showed the top part of his body, I imagined that by the way he filled out his navy blue suit that there were hard and defined muscles underneath it.

I was getting wet just looking at him.

Focus, Aubrey…Focus…

Strangely, his bio was the shortest one of them all. It didn't list his education, his background, or the year he became partner. It was just a bunch of filler words about how "the firm was so honored to have such an esteemed and proven lawyer" on their team. Oh, and he enjoyed eating chocolate.

How informative...

I copied and pasted all of their bios into a word document, and then I called Thoreau.

"Good evening, *Alyssa*," he answered, making me melt with his voice as usual. I swore he could talk me into doing anything—*almost* anything.

"Hey, um…"

"*Yes?*"

God, I loved his fucking voice... He hadn't said much of anything and I was already turned on.

"You called so I could listen to you breathe?" He had to be smiling.

"I did, actually." I rolled my eyes. "Are you enjoying my sounds?"

"I'd enjoy them a lot better if you were underneath me."

I blushed. "Um…"

"The case, Alyssa." He laughed. "Tell me about your latest case."

"Right, um…" I cleared my throat. "Long story short: My client carried a gun into a federal bank and forgot to turn on the safety lock. Someone bumped into him and his hands instinctively went to his pocket, and the gun fired—shooting him in the leg."

"Since when do you practice *criminal* law? I thought your specialty was corporate."

Shit... "It is, it is. I'm taking this case for a friend, pro bono."

"Hmmm. Well, your *friend* is looking at two to five years in a federal prison if he doesn't have any priors. What part of this do you need help with exactly?"

"The pleading part. He didn't hurt anyone but himself."

"Did he have a license to carry?"

"No…" I looked through my notes.

"Then I'm sure the prosecution will convince the jury that he carried that gun into the bank with the intent to harm someone other than *himself*. Take whatever deal they offer."

"Well, I..." I looked at what the assignment sheet said. "What if I already rejected that deal?"

He sighed. "Call the prosecution and try to get it back. If they say no, plead no contest."

"*No contest*? Are you out of your mind?"

"*Are you*? What type of corporate lawyer agrees to take an open and shut criminal case? A fairly inexperienced one at that..."

"For your information, it's an assign—" I coughed. "Never mind. Telling me to plead no contest is pretty much the same thing as telling me to plead guilty."

"If that was the case, I would have said *plead guilty*." He sounded annoyed. "*No contest* is your client's best option, and any *real* lawyer would know that. Are you sure you passed the bar exam?"

"I wouldn't have been invited to join LawyerChat if I hadn't, would I?" I felt my heart ache with that lie. "I'm just trying to avoid my client being sentenced to prison."

"Then you *really* should stick to corporate law." There was a smile in his voice. "Your client is going to prison and there's nothing you can do about it. The only negotiable thing about his case is *how long* he'll spend there. Anything else I can help you with? Do I need to lecture you on the difference between *guilty* and *not guilty*?"

I rolled my eyes and put the file away. "Thank you for your condescending help as always."

"My pleasure," he said. "I need to ask you something important."

"About my case?"

"No." He let out a low laugh. "What do you look like?"

"*What*?" I could barely hear my voice. "What did you say?"

"You heard me. Since I may never get a chance to see you, I'd like to know. *What do you look like?*"

I stood up and walked over to my mirror, letting my eyes roam over my reflection. "I'm not sure how I'm supposed to answer that…" I needed to change the subject, fast. From everything he'd told me about his dates over the past few months, he definitely had a type he liked best, a type that intrigued him like no other: Blonde, slightly curvy, full lips…

Me.

I'd tried to envision what he looked like plenty of times. Dark haired, maybe? Dirty blond? A mouth made for kissing with deep green eyes? Six pack, no, *eight pack* that leads down to a lick-able V?

He does mention working out every day…

I was more than certain that he was attractive—he had to be if so many women put up with him on those dating sites, but each time my mind drew a picture, I'd convince myself that I had him all wrong.

"You know what?" I said, snapping out of my thoughts. "I've never been good at describing things. What do *you* look like?"

"I look like a man who wants to fuck you."

Tingles ran up and down my spine. "That's not a description…"

"What color is your hair?" He didn't sound amused, and I knew he wasn't going to let me direct the conversation tonight.

"Red." I yanked the band from around my bun and let the blond strands fall to my shoulders.

"How long is it?"

"It's short…"

"Hmmm. What about your eyes?"

I stared at my blue and grey irises. "Green, light green."

"Do you have freckles?"

"No." At least that part was true.

"And your lips?"

"You want to know how thin or thick they are?"

"I want to know how they'd look wrapped around my cock."

I gasped.

"Are you playing shy tonight?" Ice cubes clinked against a glass in his background. "How much of my cock do you think you could take into your mouth?"

I remained silent, and my breathing began to slow.

"Alyssa?" His voice was soft. "Are you going to answer me?"

"It's hard to make a prediction about something you've never done." I heard him inhale a deep breath, and the line went completely silent.

I thought he'd ask me how I'd managed to have sex with boyfriends in the past without ever giving a blowjob, but he didn't.

"Hmmm. Are you a natural redhead?"

"What does it matter?" I moved over to my bed. "I'm clearly not your type."

"I have a *preference*, not a type, and a smart mouthed redhead who's never had another man's cock in her mouth is more than worthy of an exception."

I hooked a thumb underneath my panties and peeled them off before slipping under the sheets. "Too bad I'm not a full blown virgin, huh?"

"I don't fuck virgins." He paused. "But considering the fact that you and I have never fucked, you might as well be one."

Wetness slipped down my thighs, and I felt my nipples hardening. "I highly doubt—"

"I'm tired of only being able to talk to you on the phone, Alyssa…"

Silence.

"I *need* to see you…" His voice was strained. "I *need* to fuck you…"

"*Thoreau*…"

"No, *listen to me*." His tone was a warning. "I need to be buried deep inside of you, feeling your pussy throb around my cock as you scream my name—my *real* name."

A hand trailed down past my stomach and between my thighs, and my fingers began to strum my clit. Slow at first, then faster, faster with every sound of his heavy breaths in my ear.

"I've been very patient with you…" His voice trailed off. "Don't you think?"

"No…"

"I have," he said. "I'm tired of imagining how wet your pussy can get, how loudly you'll scream when I suck your tits as you ride me…How hard I'll pull your hair when I bend you over my desk and fuck you until you can't breathe…*Tired.*"

I shut my eyes, letting my other hand squeeze my breast, letting my thumb pinch my nipple.

"I'm giving you two weeks to come to your fucking senses…"

"*What?*"

"*Two weeks*," he whispered. "That's when you and I are going to meet face to face, and I'm going to claim every inch of you."

"I can't…I can't agree to…that."

"*You will.*" His breathing was now in sync with mine. "And the second you do, you're going to invite me over and I'm going to remind you of everything you've teased me with over the past six months."

I was speechless. My clit was swelling with each rub of my finger, and my breaths were getting shorter and shorter.

"I'll be gentle at first," he whispered, "especially when I slide my cock into your mouth and pull on your hair, showing you exactly how I like it to be sucked."

"*Stop…*" I was panting. "*Please…Stop…*"

"Trust me, *I won't.*"

"*Thoreau…*" My legs were trembling.

"I can't just *talk* to you anymore. I need to *feel you*, I need to *taste you*. Say yes to two weeks…"

I bit my lip, knowing that if he said it again, if he asked me one more time, I would say yes.

"*Alyssa…*" He was begging.

I was seconds away from coming, seconds away from screaming "Yes! Yes! Yes!"

"Promise me you'll let me fuck you in two weeks…"

As if my mouth was under his command, it freed my bottom lip and prepared to say yes, but I hung up.

Keeping my eyes shut, I lay in bed and let the waves of an orgasm roll through me as I screamed the three yeses he couldn't hear. When I finally stopped shaking, I rolled over and grabbed a pillow, pulling it to my chest.

Before I could force myself to sleep, I heard my phone ringing beneath me.

It was a text from Thoreau. *"I'll take that as a yes. Fourteen days."*

burden of proof (n.):

The obligation to prove or disprove a disputed fact.

Andrew

"Did I tell you that I landed the leading role for that ballet I auditioned for?" Alyssa said to me the next morning.

I'd been talking to her since I arrived at work, but I'd made no mention of the fact that she'd hung up in my face last night; I was going to punish her for that later. Severely.

Thirteen days...

"Did I tell you about it?" she asked again.

"*No,* and if you're not going to tell me when and where the show is, then I don't care."

"Oh, wow." She laughed. "You're mad about last night, aren't you?"

"*Furious.*"

"Because I hung up?"

"Because I know you screamed yes when you came, and you hung up because you didn't want me to hear it."

She was silent, and I was about to say something else, but Jessica suddenly stepped into my office, smiling at me.

"Hold on one second." I put my phone against my chest. "Yes, Jessica?"

"The final interviews are going to start in twenty minutes. They need you in the conference room now."

"I'll get there when I get there." I acted as if the kiss she was now blowing me wasn't happening, and waited until she closed the door. "I'll have to call you back later, Alyssa. I have a meeting."

"Must be bad timing for both of us. I have a meeting, too."

"Your doomed gunshot client?"

"No, something much worse. An intern interview."

"Must be in the air then." I sighed as I slipped into my jacket. "I have to sit through a few of them myself, unfortunately."

"Any advice you want to share?"

"Try to look like you're actually paying attention while they answer the questions, and make sure your cell phone is fully charged so you can get on the internet."

"Not for me." She laughed. "For the interns. Something I should say if one of them is nervous."

"Oh." I shrugged. "Tell them my motto."

"And what motto would that be?"

"It is what it is."

"Why do I ever ask you anything?"

"Because I always tell you the truth." I hung up.

"Mr. Hamilton?" Jessica stepped into my office again. "They want you to look over the files before they begin."

"I'm right behind you." I followed her into the conference room, where Will Greenwood and George Bach were waiting, and I sat next to them.

"Good to see you out of your office today, Andrew." Will laughed.

"Yeah," George added. "Thank you for bestowing your presence upon us this afternoon. We know how much you *love* being sociable."

I rolled my eyes. "Why do the three of us need to conduct intern interviews? What's the purpose of having an HR department if *the partners* do their job for them?"

"This is a *family*, Andrew." Mr. Greenwood spoke sternly. "Whether it's an intern, the secretary, or the young man who stays overnight and cleans this office, I want everyone to feel like they're a part of a huge family. Don't you?"

"I'm not answering that," I said. "How many are we picking this year?"

"Not too many." Will slid me a folder. "We have our top five picks. We just need to narrow it down to three. Two from law school, one from pre-law. We'll add two more next semester."

"Hmmm." I pulled out the applications and pretended to pay attention as the two of them went over each applicant's achievements.

"Okay, Jessica!" Will pressed the intercom button. "You can send in the first applicant!"

When the door opened, I expected to see the usual plainly dressed stiff with a wooden smile, but the woman who stepped inside was far from that. Dressed in a light grey dress that clung to her hips and a pair of nude high heels, she was one of the sexiest women I'd ever seen; I couldn't take my eyes off her.

Her eyes were a deep ocean blue that matched the sapphire necklace hanging around her neck. Her hair was pulled into a low ponytail—the loose strands slightly grazed her breasts, and her lips—her bright pink, fuck-able lips, seemed to be mouthing words of some kind.

I have no idea what you're saying...

As I was noticing the pink bra strap that had slipped from underneath her dress and onto her bare shoulder, her stunning eyes met mine. I raised my eyebrow and she blushed. Then she immediately turned away, looking at my partners.

"Welcome to GBH, Miss Everhart," George said. "We're happy that you're here for an interview, but as you know we can only select *one* undergraduate intern for our program at this time."

"I understand, sir." Her eyes met mine again, and my cock twitched.

I tried to stop the images that were flooding my brain, images of me bending this woman over the table, fucking her against my office wall, and tying her hands above her head and torturing her with my tongue all night, but they wouldn't stop. Each image dissolved into another one, and before I knew it, I'd visually undressed her and there was no one in this room but the two of us.

What the hell is wrong with me? Attracted to a prospective intern? An UNDERGRADUATE intern?

"Well, let's get started then." George interrupted my thoughts. "Mr. Hamilton, would you care to start with the first question?"

"Not particularly," I said, trying to ignore the fact that Miss Everhart was smoothing her dress over her thighs.

He nudged me under the table and whispered under his breath, "Family, Andrew...*Family*."

I rolled my eyes. "Why do you want to be a lawyer, Miss Everhart?"

"I enjoy screwing people over," she said. "I figure I might as well get paid for it."

My lips curved into a smile, and George and Will laughed.

"In all seriousness, gentlemen," she continued, "I come from a large family of lawyers and judges; it's what I've known my whole life. I know the justice system is far from perfect, but nothing makes me happier than seeing it at its best. There's no greater feeling than working for the good of society."

"Good answer," Will said. "Now, we're going to ask you a series of questions regarding the real-world case study packets that we mailed you. Were you able to complete everything?"

"Yes, sir."

"Great. Question number one: Your client walks into a federal bank with a loaded gun in his pocket. Upon being brushed by a stranger, the gun fires—shooting him in the leg. Regarding the charges that the prosecution filed, how would you have your client plead?"

"*What?*" I looked over at him. "Could you repeat that question, Will?"

"The prompt?"

"Whatever you just asked."

He nodded and happily repeated it, putting extra emphasis on the crime of walking into a bank with a loaded firearm.

My mind immediately flashed back to the conversation I'd had with Alyssa last night.

I smiled, thinking that maybe Alyssa's "friend" was a headline story in the local news, that maybe I could figure out who she was without her telling me. I pulled out my phone and held it underneath the conference table, googling "Man shoots himself in federal bank. North Carolina."

Nothing relevant appeared.

Hmmm...

"How would you make him plead, Miss Everhart?" Will asked again.

"No contest," she said quickly.

"*No contest?*" He sounded slightly impressed. "Why so?"

"He doesn't have a license to carry, so I'm sure the prosecution will try to make it seem like he carried that gun into the bank for a reason. Regardless of if he only hurt himself, he's looking at a prison sentence, so we could bypass the trial and try to limit it to the lowest terms possible."

I blinked, refusing to believe that her answer was anything more than a coincidence. As a matter of fact, as soon as she started to further explain her logic, I knew that it was; only a student would start talking about "emotional appeal" right after a no contest plea.

As Will and George continued to pepper her with questions, I googled variations of that federal gun case. "Man fires gun in bank." "No contest plea in federal bank case." "Man injures himself in bank shooting."

Still, nothing.

"Miss Everhart, are there any lawyers that you wish to model your own career after?" Greg asked.

"Yes, actually," she said. "I've always admired the career of Liam Henderson."

"*Liam Henderson?*" I raised my eyebrow. "Who is that?" Usually, interviewees named a federal judge, a well-known prosecutor, or a familiar district attorney. But an unknown? Never.

"Well, he made history as the youngest lawyer to ever uncover a government conspiracy, and he—"

I tuned out her answer. I'd just thought of another phrase to google.

"Interesting choice, Miss Everhart," Will said. "Do you have any current mentors in the law profession besides your family members?"

"I do."

"Are you in close contact with this mentor? If so, how often?"

"We talk almost every day, so I'd like to think that we're close."

Why isn't this case popping up? If it's a "federal" bank shooting, it should be plastered all over the papers...

"Would your mentor be able to speak to us, or send a letter regarding your character?" Will was definitely impressed with this woman, and she had this job. The second set of questions he had yet to ask weren't really necessary.

"I'm sure I could ask him to do that if need be," she said just as I was starting a new web search.

"Great. So, tell us, what's the last bit of advice that your mentor gave you?"

I looked at my watch. As soon as today's interviews were over, I was going to call Alyssa about this case. Maybe she'd fudged some of the details to continue shrouding her identity.

"When I told him I was nervous about my interview today," Miss Everhart said softly, "he told me, *it is what it is.*"

My head immediately shot up.

"Did he now?" George clutched his chest, laughing. "That sounds like something our Andrew would say!" He patted me on the shoulder. "Isn't that right, Andrew?"

"*Yes.*" I narrowed my eyes at 'Miss Everhart.' "That sounds *exactly* like something I would say..."

She tucked a loose strand of hair behind her ear. "I'll be sure to tell my mentor that someone actually enjoys his odd sense of humor."

"*Please do.*" I watched as she answered the next questions with ease, as she barely blinked her big blue eyes when the questions became tougher. And the more I heard her talk, the more I heard the familiarities of her speech pattern, I had to force myself not to fucking lose it.

One coincidence was fine, but two? Damn near unfathomable.

As they asked her about her favorite inspirational quotes, I scrolled down to Alyssa's number and dialed. I knew for a fact that she *never* silenced her phone for some strange reason, and I had to know if what I was thinking was true, or if my mind was playing a cruel joke on me.

I could see the rings on my phone's screen, see the seconds as they passed, and when it rang three times, I let out a huge sigh of relief. But then the sound of bell chimes filled the room.

"I am so sorry." Miss Everhart's cheeks turned pink and she picked up her purse. "I have a weird thing about never putting this on silent...I really meant to leave it in my car." She pulled out her phone, slightly smiling once she looked at the screen, and then she hit ignore.

WHAT. THE. FUCK!

"Happens all the time." Will laughed. "We were going on and on anyway. It's a good thing it went off so we can close out with the final questions. Anything from you, Andrew?"

I glared at 'Alyssa'. I was confused, pissed, and unfortunately aroused all at once.

"Andrew?"

"*No*," I said, noticing that she was blushing again. "I have absolutely nothing to say."

Will and Greg both stood up and smiled, reaching out to shake her hand, but I remained seated.

I couldn't believe this shit.

She wasn't a green-eyed redhead like she'd said over the phone, *far* from being a licensed lawyer, and she was a *fucking liar*...

"Mr. Hamilton?" She was standing in front of me with her hand outstretched. "Thank you for interviewing me today. It was an absolute pleasure meeting you."

"The pleasure's all mine." I shook her hand, trying my best to ignore the smooth softness of her touch. "Good luck."

She nodded, said goodbye to the three of us once more, and then she left the room.

As Will and George discussed how impressed they were with her interview, I forced myself to look through her file.

Double major student at Duke: Pre-law and Ballet. Perfect 4.0 GPA. Recently cast as the lead of *Swan Lake*, recently listed in the top ten percent of her class. There were *ten* letters of recommendation in her folder—all from impeccable lawyers; there was even one from the newly appointed assistant district attorney.

As amazing as her personal accomplishments were, it was her birthdate that stood out to me the most. She was twenty two.

Twenty fucking two.

And, even though she was the most accomplished out of all the undergraduates, she wasn't even a senior.

She was a *junior*...

I ignored Alyssa's text tonight, the one that read, *"If you haven't found another unfortunate date for tonight, call me when you see this."*

I was too angry to say anything to her. After all the hours we'd spent on the phone, all the times that I'd told her that I hated liars, she'd lied to me. Repeatedly.

I'd wanted to vote no for her employment, but I couldn't bring myself to do it. Once we'd finished with the last interview of the day, the decision on the top pick was unanimous: Aubrey Everhart.

Yet, while they frenziedly weighed the pros and cons of the other applicants, I sat there in a daze—angry with myself for not seeing through all of Aubrey's lies earlier.

In the six months that we'd spoken, she'd always asked questions that were a little too simple, questions that sometimes made me wonder, but I never thought twice about it. She'd mentioned Duke University a few times, but she never talked about it for long and she always made it seem as if she'd graduated from there. But her constant talk of how she wanted her parents' approval and had conflicted feelings between choosing dance and the law should have been a dead ass giveaway.

At this point, I wasn't sure which lie to be more upset about: The fact that she wasn't a lawyer, the fact that she was still in college, or the fact that she'd lied about her physical appearance.

Pouring my sixth shot of the night, I realized that that last lie—although irrelevant in the grand scheme of things, was the one that hit me the hardest. She was definitely my 'type,' and the second she walked into that interview I wanted her, before I found out who she really was, before I found out her age.

Tossing back a shot, I heard my phone ringing. *Her.*

I rolled my eyes and let it sit on the table. I grabbed one of my last Cuban cigars and stepped out onto my balcony. I needed to think.

The sky was starless tonight—nearly pitch black, and the moon was hiding underneath a curtain of dark clouds. As much as I didn't want to admit it, tonight's sky bore a horrid resemblance to a certain night that occurred six years ago.

It was the night my life changed forever, the night that left me broken, shattered, and numb. All because of lies—a series of heartbreaking and inconceivable lies.

I tried hard to prevent myself from picturing the memories, but I could still hear that strained, ragged voice in my head: "*Andrew... You have to help me... You have to get me out of here... Please... Save me, Andrew...*"

I shook my head and blocked out the rest of that memory. Unlike six years ago, I was in control of this situation, and "Alyssa" lying to me meant that our friendship was over, done.

There was no justification for what she'd done, but before I cut her off, I needed to make her pay for lying to me, and I needed to figure out *how*.

conviction (n.):

A judgment of guilt against a criminal defendant.

Andrew

"Mr. Hamilton?" Aubrey set my coffee down on my desk two weeks later. I'd *personally* insisted that she work as my intern, even though looking at her made me angry.

I'd made a point not to say too much around her, to refrain from staring at her too long, and I couldn't help being crueler than ever—dismissive even. I made her responsible for my daily coffee, demanded that she re-do every assignment at least three times, and whenever she asked for my help, I answered her with a detached "Figure it out yourself."

She never seemed upset or offended by my harshness, which made me even angrier. I'd thought that by having her work for me and seeing her crack under pressure that my attraction to her would fade, but it only intensified each time I saw her face.

Especially today.

As I pulled my coffee closer, I noticed that her nipples were poking through her thin, beige dress, and it was so tight that I could see the imprint of lace panties.

Fuck...

"Mr. Hamilton?" she asked again.

"Yes, Miss Everhart?"

"I have an important rehearsal for a ballet I'm a part of, so I was wondering..." She looked absolutely nervous. "Can I go home early today?"

"*No.*"

She sighed. "I really need to be at this rehearsal...It's at the Grand Hall."

"So?"

"*So,*" she said, clearing her throat, "with all due respect, *Mr. Hamilton*, this is a pretty big deal for me. The Grand Hall is usually reserved for performances, so for them to open it and let us use it for a rehearsal is—"

I wasn't listening, and as much as I wanted to look at my work again and make it clear that she was being ignored, I couldn't. I was too busy staring at the contours of her mouth.

"That's a fact." She was still talking for some reason. "I think I've made very valid points, and since I'm not asking for too much, you should agree to let me go."

"Get back to work, Miss Everhart."

"Mr. Hamilton, please—"

"Get. Back. To. Work." I glared at her, daring her to let another word slip out of her seductive mouth. "I don't care about your personal life. I pay you for twenty five hours a week, so you'll work *twenty five hours a week*, and you'll work them when I say you'll work them. So, get back to your cubicle."

She stared at me for a few seconds, and I couldn't help but notice tears welling in her eyes.

"You can take that box of Kleenex with you on your way out," I said.

Shaking her head, she stepped back and headed for the door. "I'm going to ask Mr. Bach if I can leave early. No disrespect to you."

"*Excuse me*?" I stood up. "What did you just say?"

She continued to walk toward the door, the sound of her heels clicking faster and faster. Before she could turn the knob, I spun her around and slammed my hand against the door.

"I'm not a fan of insubordination, Miss Everhart."

"You won't have to worry about that anymore." Her face was red, twisted in anger. ""I'm going to ask Mr. Bach to move me with someone else because I refuse to work with you anymore."

"Good luck with that. No one else wanted you. *Only me.*"

"I highly doubt that." She tried to move away, but I grabbed her hands and pinned them above her head.

"I was the best interviewee and you fucking know it." She hissed. "And since we both know that's a fact, I don't have to put up with your shit anymore." She looked as if she wanted to spit in my face. "You are a cruel, cold, and condescending asshole, and I haven't learned shit from you; I doubt I ever will."

"Watch your goddamn mouth. I'm still your boss."

"You *were* my boss."

I tightened my grasp around her wrists and looked directly into her eyes, pressing my chest against her breasts. "Let me tell you what's about to happen, *Aubrey*. You're going to go back to your cubicle and you're going to stay there until you're done for the day—only getting up to bring me a new cup of coffee. You will tell your ballet director that you'll come after you get your work done, and you will not go to Mr. Bach and say anything, because we don't reassign interns just because they cry."

"Then I guess there's a first time for everything." She threw my glares right back at me, narrowing her eyes as her chest heaved up and down.

"Aubrey—"

"Let me go before I *scream*, Mr. Hamilton. I wasn't listening to a thing you just said so I highly suggest—"

I crashed my lips against hers, effectively making her shut the hell up. I kept my hands tightly clamped around her wrists, pressing her body against the door with my hips.

She murmured as I slipped my tongue into her mouth, as I bit her bottom lip as hard as I could. Without thinking, I let her hands go and gripped her waist—pulling her taut against me as my hand found its way underneath her skirt.

I slid my hand across the crotch of her panties, tapping my fingers against the lace, and then I slowly pushed them to the side and plunged a finger deep into her pussy.

"Ahhh..." she moaned, making me bite her lip again, making me use two fingers instead of one.

She was wet—*soaking wet*, and as much as I wanted to fuck her senseless against my door and make her forget her name, I tore my mouth away from her.

"Get the hell out of my office."

"*What?*" She asked breathlessly, her eyes widening in surprise.

"Go to your *important* rehearsal."

"Mr. Ham—"

"Hurry up before I change my mind." I reached around her and opened the door. "*Go.*"

She didn't hesitate to walk past me, and as soon as she was gone I knew damn well this arrangement wasn't going to work for too much longer. Either she was going to be reassigned or I was going to have to fire her, fast.

Hours later, when I was halfway through my work for the day, I noticed I'd received a new text from Alyssa. I rolled my eyes and changed her name to Aubrey before reading it.

"*Where have you been for the past two weeks?*" it said. "*Are you okay? I've called and texted you and you haven't said anything. I'm really concerned...If you get this, say something, anything.*"

I didn't want to respond, but with the taste of her mouth still lingering on my lips, I gave in. "*I'm fine. Just made a major* discovery not too long ago and I've been trying to figure out how to deal with it."

"Is it something serious?"

"VERY serious."

"I'm sorry...Want to know something that will make you feel better?"

"I doubt anything you say can do that right now."

"Want to bet?"

"Try me."

"My boss just kissed the shit out of me. I think that's why he's so damn mean to me; he wants to fuck me..."

"I really don't think your 'boss' wants to fuck you..."

"He definitely does. His cock was rock hard when he was kissing me, and he was biting my lips and gripping me like he wanted to own me... I've never been so wet in my life..."

I hesitated. "How exactly is this supposed to make me feel better?"

"I was pretending he was you the whole time. I miss you."

I immediately turned off my phone. I didn't know what type of shit she was trying to pull, but I wasn't falling for it.

"I was pretending it was you? I miss you?" Bullshit.

I wasn't going to answer her calls or her messages for a long time. Sexy ass mouth or not.

cross examination (n.):

The interrogation of a witness called by one's opponent.

Aubrey

I couldn't stop thinking about the way Mr. Hamilton kissed me the other day, the way he pulled me against his chest and fucked my lips with his mouth.

Thoughts of him kissing me had been invading my mind all day, and even now, when I was setting down his latest cup of coffee, I was tempted to walk behind his desk and dare him to kiss me again. Ever since I'd become his intern, he'd been quite mean to me—reckless, but I thought it was a training technique, a way to see if I'd quit under pressure.

Until he kissed me that day.

There was something intangible in his kiss; unspoken words, a repressed desire. It made me think that the glances he often tossed my way, those looks of scorn that were laced with wanting, meant a little more.

I placed a plastic stirrer into his cup and cleared my throat. "Do you need anything else, Mr. Hamilton?"

No answer.

I stood my ground and waited for him to look up at me; I wanted to see his face.

The suit he was wearing today—a dark grey three piece with a silver silk tie, made him look even more devastatingly beautiful than he normally did.

"Is there a problem, Miss Everhart?" He clenched his fists above the desk, trying his best to act like my presence wasn't bothering him. But it was, I could tell.

I knew he would look up at any moment, so I stepped back, making sure the light blue dress I wore specifically for him would be in full view, but he kept his gaze lowered.

"No, sir."

"Then get out of my office. I'll need your Brownstein report with my next cup of coffee. Four o' clock."

"You just gave me that report yesterday. You said I could take all the time I needed."

"You must've misheard me. You can take all the time you need *today*. Things change instantly around here, and that's the exact reason why some of us never leave early. Four o' clock."

I stood there completely speechless. There was no way I'd be able to read and summarize a three hundred paged report by the end of the day.

"Did you lose some of your hearing between today and yesterday?" He finally looked up, his perfect face expressionless. "I need complete silence when I work and I can't focus with your heavy breathing." He narrowed his eyes at me. "Get out, finish the report, and bring it back to me with my coffee. If you don't, you're fired."

I quickly decided that he was bipolar, and that our seemingly connected kiss was just a mistake. I turned around and left his office, rushing straight to the break room.

There was no way I was going to get that Brownstein report done by the end of the day.

I pulled out my phone and scrolled through my messages—realizing that Thoreau hadn't responded to my morning texts.

Sighing, I decided to call him. I needed someone to tell me that my life wouldn't end today when I was fired.

It rang once.

It rang twice.

It went to voicemail.

He hit ignore?!

I sent him a text. *"What the hell is wrong with you lately? Is your lack of sex forcing you to act like a jerk toward me? Is the withdrawal THAT BAD? Talk to me."*

I waited for a response, but none came, so I slumped onto the couch. There was no point in even attempting to finish that report. I was just going to sit here, relax, and when it was five o' clock I was going to collect all of my things and leave.

I could find another internship in two weeks, or worst case, ask the department chair if I could shadow my mother and father around their stuffy firm for credit.

Ugh…God…

I shut my eyes and lay back against the cushion, wishing I could fall asleep.

"Aubrey?" Someone shook my shoulder just as I was drifting away.

"Yes?" I opened my eyes. It was Jessica.

"I've been looking for you forever. Mr. Hamilton wants to speak with you."

I raised my eyebrow. "More coffee?"

"Probably." She shrugged. "He's been a bit off lately. Just come on, you don't want to make him angry." She held the door open and I stood up, making my way past her.

I debated whether I should even go to his office. Then again, seeing the look on his face as I said, "Fuck you. I quit." was too good of an experience to pass up. I forced a smile and knocked on his door.

"Come in." His voice was stern.

I slipped inside, expecting to see him holding an empty coffee cup, but he was sitting at his desk–glaring at me.

"Have a seat," he said.

I sat in front of his desk, waiting for him to scold me about something, to unleash more of his seemingly bipolar tendencies, but he didn't. He just kept staring at me.

I hated the effect he was having on my body right now, and as much as I wanted to ask him what the hell he wanted, I couldn't get my mouth to say a thing.

∆"Lawyers are supposed to be people with integrity, are they not?" he whispered.

"Yes."

"Do you think *you* have integrity, *Miss Everhart*?" He emphasized every syllable of my name.

"Yes."

"Hmmm." He leaned forward. "So, would you ever willingly withhold the truth from someone you supposedly cared about?"

"It depends..." My breath hitched in my throat; my heart was racing a mile a minute.

"It *depends*?" He sat back a bit. "It depends on what?"

"If the truth would damage anything or hurt someone unnecessarily, then I believe I have a right to withhold it."

"But what if someone blatantly asked you for the truth, several times? What if he said, I want you to tell me the truth no matter how much it hurts, or how angry it may make me?"

Where is he going with this? "Are you referring to a potential witness changing his testimony on the stand, Mr. Hamilton?"

"No..." He trailed his fingers across my collarbone, setting my nerves on fire. "This is a *personal* inquiry. I'm just in need of an outside opinion. Answer the question."

"Well, I think—" I sucked in a breath as he placed his hand on my thigh and strummed his fingers against my skirt. "I think certain lies have to be told, and certain truths have to be withheld. The ultimate conviction is up to those who can discern which is which."

"So, you believe in reasonable doubt?"

"In certain cases, yes..."

"What about in *our* case?" His hand was slowly slipping underneath my skirt, traveling further and further up my thigh.

"*Our* case?"

"Yes," he said. "I believe you and I are currently in an unfortunate web of deceit."

"No..." I said, breathless and confused. "We're not in a web of deceit..."

"We definitely are, *Alyssa*—" He pulled me forward by the strand of pearls around my neck. "It's the case of a woman who befriended me online, but she turned out to be someone completely different than who she told me she was. So, in this case— *our case*, how do you feel about reasonable doubt?"

Gasping, I could feel all the color draining from my face. My heart wasn't racing anymore; it was flailing around wildly— ready to jump out of my chest, and my eyes were as wide as they could go.

"You were very good at covering your tracks for such a long time, so I'll give you that," he said. "But I thought we thoroughly discussed how I felt about liars. Did we not?"

I murmured as he tightened his grip on my pearls, as he pulled me so close that we were lip to lip.

"Do you plan on answering me, *Aubrey*? Are you tired of this fucking charade?"

"I never thought that..." I was stuttering, trying to look away from him, but his grip prevented me from moving. "I am so sorry..."

He didn't say anything further. He stared into my eyes, searching for something that wasn't there. Then he lowered his voice, and leaned back. "Once someone lies to me they're dead to me forever. Do you remember me saying that?"

"Yes…"

"So, you've always been willing to lose our friendship over lies?"

"I never wanted to meet you in person…"

"I can see that." He hissed.

"If I had known who you really were…" I was breaking down in front of him. This was too much for one day. "I would've never—"

"Save it." He cut me off. "I've heard enough about your thoughts on *lying*. Seeing as though we don't share the same views, you're not worthy of being my intern. You'll be serving as my secretary's assistant until further notice."

"You're *demoting* me?"

"It's not a demotion. It's a way to keep you out of my sight."

My heart dropped.

"Our online relationship—whatever the hell that was anyway," he said, "is over. I don't want to hear from you outside of these walls again."

"*Thoreau…*"

"It's Mr. Hamilton, *Miss Everhart*." He glared at me. "Mr. fucking Hamilton."

"You have to believe that I'm sorry…I never thought that this would happen."

"Take however much time you need on the Brownstein account." He disregarded my apology and released his hold on my necklace. "You have until the end of next week. And from now on, you can just set my coffee on my bookcase. I don't need you coming anywhere near my desk."

"Andrew—"

"We are definitely *not* on a first name basis. Do not ever call me that."

"Just let me explain…"

"There's nothing *to* explain. You lied to me and you no longer exist. Get out. Now."

I felt tears welling in my eyes. "I was serious about you being my only friend…Friends are supposed to give each other a chance to make things right. Just let me tell you why I had to lie to you…"

"I don't deal with liars. *Ever*. And seeing that that's exactly what you are, I don't care why you felt the need to deceive me. Get out of my office, stay out of my sight as much as possible, and do your damn job."

I stood up and looked into his eyes, pleading for him to simply hear me out, to let me explain, but he turned away from me. Then he picked up his phone.

"Jessica?" he said. "Could you help Miss Everhart find her way out of my office? And could you please have the janitor check my floors for fucking superglue?"

I stood underneath the scalding hot streams of my shower, crying. Right after I'd left Andrew's office, I'd told HR that I wasn't feeling well and needed to leave for the rest of the day.

I'd driven straight for the dance hall—locking myself into a private room and dancing until I couldn't feel my feet anymore. I knew I must've looked crazy to my classmates, sobbing in between every twirl, but I didn't care; I needed to clear my mind of all thoughts of Andrew, Thoreau, and Alyssa.

As the water continued to lash against my skin, I shut my eyes and murmured, "How long has he known?" I thought about the past couple weeks, how "Thoreau" had been less talkative than normal, how he'd ignored me, and then it hit me.

My interview…

I still remembered it because seeing Andrew in person made me realize that no picture could ever accurately capture how sexy he really looked, and I'd blushed the second his eyes met mine. He didn't seem to act any differently throughout the questioning, but then I remembered that random phone call...

I wasn't sure why I was just remembering it now, but while Mr. Bach and Mr. Greenwood had simply laughed that intrusive phone call away, Andrew had stared at me. As if he was in complete and utter shock. And at the end of the interview, when I'd reached for his hand, his gaze wasn't intrigued anymore, it was heated.

Wiping away my tears, I turned off the water and stepped out. I wrapped myself in a towel and did what I always did when I felt sad: ordered a sandwich and made myself a couple of stiff martinis.

Just as I was downing the first one, there was a knock on my door. I noticed the pink Barbie keys on the counter—courtesy of my forgetful and "never here" roommate and knew it was her.

She always leaves something...

"Would it kill you to double check for these before you—" I stopped when I opened the door.

It was Andrew, and the look on his face was one of pure anger. He wasn't dressed in a suit anymore, just a simple, thin white T-shirt that slightly clung to his chiseled abs and a pair of faded blue jeans.

I tried to slam the door in his face, but he held it open and forced himself inside my apartment. I started to step backwards and he matched me step for step, backing me against my living room wall.

"We need to talk." His voice was flat, emotionless.

"No, we don't. You said plenty earlier." I looked down at the floor. "Don't worry, I'll be resigning in the morning. Please leave."

He tilted my chin up and looked into my eyes. "You're not quitting."

"*Watch me*." I swallowed. "I want you to leave…"

"I would believe that, but you say things you don't mean all the time."

The tension between us was damn near palpable, and I could feel my blood heating every second he stood there staring at me. I tried to move away, but he gripped my hips.

"You told me you were a lawyer, Aubrey…" he said, his voice dripping with malice. "You told me you were twenty seven years old."

"I never *said* I was twenty seven. You assumed."

"It was on your fucking profile!" He pushed my back against the wall. "You never thought to correct me whenever I said I was only five years older than you…I'm *ten years* older than you."

"I didn't think I would ever meet you in person," I barely managed to say as he pressed his chest against mine.

"That excuses your *lies*?"

"I said I was sorry, and it was clearly a huge mistake to ever befriend you. You didn't even give me a chance to completely explain."

"Do you not understand how *fucked up* this situation is?"

"No…" I murmured as our lips touched.

"I've been looking forward to fucking the woman who teased me every night for nearly six months," he whispered, sliding his fingers underneath my towel. "I wanted her to ride me." He trailed his hand up my thigh and rubbed his thumb against my clit. "On my cock and my mouth. And I wanted to teach her how to taste me…Don't you think this woman fucked all of that up?"

I shook my head in response; I couldn't handle the way he was looking at me.

"You said you weren't my type when I asked what you looked like." He pulled away from my mouth, but he kept his thumb against my clit. "But you clearly *are*. Why did you lie about something as simple as that?""

"You didn't tell me what you looked like, so—"

"Stop *deflecting*." He hissed, and took a step back. "Tell me the reasoning. I've already figured out your reasoning for the other bullshit lies. By the way, no self-respecting lawyer would *ever* let another lawyer do their work for them."

"Only a self-absorbed asshole who wants to seem deeper than he really is would call himself *Thoreau*."

"Good to finally see the version of you that I remember." He took another step back and crossed his arms. "Answer my question."

"*Fuck you*." I scoffed. "I told you I was sorry, begged you to listen to me, and now when *you* feel like talking, you think you can barge into my apartment and *make me*?"

"I haven't *made you* do anything." He smirked. "*Yet*."

Silence.

He leaned against the wall, waiting for me to speak, but I couldn't get a word out.

Look away from him…Look away from him…

As if he knew the power his gaze was having on me, he grinned and picked up one of my makeshift martinis.

Lifting one of the cherries from the liquor, he placed it against his lips. "Do you plan on standing there all night and looking at me, or are you going to answer my question?"

"No," I said, finally looking away from him. "After the way you treated me in your office today, I don't owe you a goddamn thing. You can stand there all night for all I care." I walked towards my room. "There's even a sandwich delivery coming if you decide to—"

My breath caught in my throat as he grabbed me from behind and pulled me against his chest. He quickly spun me around so we were face to face, and then he ripped my towel from around my body, letting it fall to the floor.

The cherry he'd picked up was in his mouth, and he was pressing it on my lips—silently commanding me to open up and eat it.

I stuck out my tongue to take it, but before sliding it to me, he whispered, "Don't chew…I want to see how capable you are of *swallowing.*"

My gasping did all the swallowing for me.

"Good girl," he said, loosening his grip around my waist. "Now, step back and hold the wall."

"*What?*"

He pushed me against the wall before I could take another breath, grabbing my hands and lifting them above my head. "*Hold the wall…*"

I nodded, pressing my hands against the cool surface.

With a 'don't-fuck-with-me' look on his face, he sucked my bottom lip into his mouth, and spoke softly, "I'll make you regret it if you let go."

"Yes…"

"That wasn't a question." The look on his face softened, and I was sure he could hear the loud beating in my chest.

I shut my eyes as he ran his hands up and down my sides.

I could feel his cock hardening through his pants as he lowered his kisses to my breasts and swirled his tongue around my nipples.

His mouth trailed down my stomach, and his hands caressed every inch of me as he made his way down.

"*Thoreau…*" I gasped as his tongue skimmed the inside of my thighs.

"My name is *Andrew.*" He got down on his knees. "We're done playing that game." He trapped my legs with his hands and pressed his mouth against my pussy. Licking me gently, he massaged my clit with his thumb.

I tried not to moan too loudly, tried to keep it all in, but each time he swirled his tongue, my mouth let another sound escape.

"You're so fucking wet..." He groaned. "*So fucking wet...*" He slipped two thick fingers inside of me, pushing them as far as they could go.

My eyes fluttered open as he added a third finger, as he whispered, "*So tight...*"

"*Ahhh...Andrew...*" I gave up trying to be quiet.

"*Yes?*" He slowly pulled his fingers out of me and looked up, waiting for me to say something, but I couldn't focus when he looked at me liked that.

With no lead-in kisses whatsoever, he buried his head in my pussy and fucking devoured me.

"*Ohhh...*" I cried out in indescribable pleasure. "Ohhh godddd, Andrewww....Waitttt...Slow down..."

He ignored me, plunging his tongue deeper and deeper.

I couldn't help but let go of the wall. I dropped my hands to his head, grabbing fistfuls of his hair to keep my balance. The harder I pulled his hair, the more his tongue lashed against me with no mercy.

Suddenly, there was a loud knock at the door, but Andrew didn't bother stopping. Instead, he lifted my right leg up and draped it over his shoulder. He grasped my thigh so I couldn't move, and then he slid his tongue into me a little deeper—licking every corner of my walls.

On the verge of coming, I grabbed his shoulders as my pussy throbbed against his mouth. But he stopped abruptly.

He moved my leg and kissed his way back up my body, stopping when he reached my breasts. He palmed them with one hand and roughly twisted my nipples.

"I told you not to let go of that wall," he said, looking down at me as he unzipped his pants.

I stared back into his eyes, nearly breathless.

"I did tell you that, *didn't I?*" He clasped my hand and pressed it against his chest, slowly moving it lower and lower.

When my hand finally reached his dick, I looked down in utter shock. He was huge, massively thick, and my jaw was hanging wide open.

"You don't like it?" He tilted my chin up and smirked.

I was utterly speechless, but I couldn't deny how horny I felt right now. Remembering what he'd said on the phone, I lowered my head to taste him, but he stopped me.

"*Not tonight.*" He pulled a condom out of his pocket, and kept his eyes on me as he put it on.

Leading me to the couch, he sat down and pulled me into his lap.

I leaned forward to kiss his lips, but he quickly repositioned me so I was facing away from him. Then he teased me with the head of his cock—rubbing it against my slit. Again and again.

"Remember how you said you wanted to ride me until I came inside of you?" he whispered into my ear. "How you wanted to grind on me until I begged you to stop?"

"*Yes…*" I moaned.

He pushed me down by my shoulders and sank me onto his cock, burying himself to the hilt inch by inch. The further I slipped onto him, the more he groaned. The more he said my name.

When he was completely inside of me, he held me still and pressed his lips against the back of my neck, letting me adjust to his length.

The feel of him was like nothing I'd ever felt before. It was intense, powerful, *addictive*.

"*Ride me, Aubrey…*" He pushed me forward. "Fucking ride me…"

I took a deep breath and rocked against him, slowly stretching my insides further and further. I could barely maintain a rhythm; the fullness of him was almost too much, and he was rubbing my clit with his thumb—driving me insane.

"You feel so fucking good right now…" He yanked me back by my hair. "Don't fucking stop."

I held onto his legs to steady myself, slightly lifting my body up and down. I tried to finally establish a tempo, to finally take control.

"*Andrewww…*" I couldn't handle his cock anymore. "I'm… I'm about to cum…"

"*No.*" He gripped my hips harder than ever. "*Not yet.*"

He suddenly stood up, with me still impaled on his cock, and bent me over. "Grab that table and don't let go."

My fingers clutched the edge of the coffee table and he pounded into me again and again, smacking my ass each time I cried out.

"I told you I was going to *own* your pussy," he whispered harshly. "Don't cum until I tell you to fucking cum…" His cock was throbbing inside of me, and my muscles were clenching with his every stroke.

"Fuck….Fuckkkk!" My legs were starting to give out as an intense pressure built inside of me, as he fucked me relentlessly. "Andrewwwww…"

"*Don't let go.*" He warned, but I couldn't help it.

My orgasm took ahold of me in a rush and I collapsed, falling forward. Before I could land face first onto the coffee table, he pulled me back and continued pounding into me until he reached his own release.

I shut my eyes and leaned back against him, panting heavily as we both tried to catch our breath. Several minutes later, Andrew gently lifted my hips and pulled out of me.

He stood up, and I watched him as he walked into the kitchen and threw the condom away. He picked my fallen towel up from the floor and walked back over to me.

I made no move to get up, but I re-wrapped the towel around myself.

"Is there anything you *didn't* lie to me about?" His voice was a whisper.

"Yes…"

"And what would that be?"

"I did miss you…"

He raised his eyebrow, keeping the rest of his face stoic. Expressionless. He started to buckle his pants, not taking his eyes off mine.

I was hoping that he would say something, *anything*, but he didn't.

He smoothed his shirt with his hands and walked to the door. All of a sudden, he stopped and glanced over his shoulder. Then he walked over to me and lightly kissed my lips—brushing his thumb against my cheek.

I wanted to speak, to ask what he was thinking, but he pulled away and left.

This time he was gone.

recess (n.):

Temporary withdrawal or cessation from
the usual work or activity.

Andrew

I'd broken a lot of rules in my life, but sleeping with an intern was probably one of the worst ones. There was no precedent for this, and that terrified me.

The second I left Aubrey's apartment, I did what I normally did after fucking someone I met online: I went home, showered, poured a glass of my favorite scotch, and pulled out my laptop—preparing to search for the next.

Except this time, I didn't want to search for a next. I wanted to fuck Aubrey, again and again. I wanted to hear her scream a little louder, feel her body wrapped against mine, and see her face as I buried myself deep inside of her.

Damn...

I couldn't believe this. I could count on one hand the number of women I'd thought about after I left a hotel, and it wasn't because any of them were memorable in a *good* way. And the ones that *were* good, were just "good"—never amazing, like Aubrey.

A part of me felt bad for leaving her right after we finished, for not saying a word, but I *had* to leave.

I didn't do pillow talk conversations after sex. Ever.

Even though I was more than tempted to drive back over there right now and claim her again, I had to make myself accept a very harsh fact: I was never going to sleep with her again. It was against my rules.

"Where is my coffee, Jessica?" I called her desk. "Why hasn't Miss Everhart brought it to me yet? Is she late today?"

"No, sir." She sounded confused. "It's only seven thirty…"

I looked at the clock on my wall and sighed before ending the call. I was on edge for some reason, and I didn't like it.

I'd failed to get any sleep the night before and I'd purposely ignored Aubrey's midnight text. It'd read, *"Can't sleep…Can we talk about what just happened between us?"*

The answer was *no*.

Our conversations were long over. There was nothing more we had to discuss.

We talked. We fucked. That was the end of us.

I pulled up the Dating-Match website, determined to get her out of my mind. All I needed to do was find someone else, and she would become a drop in the sea of other endless women—a fleeting memory that I would halfway remember whenever I saw her gorgeous face.

There were hundreds of new women on the site now, but very few of them caught my eye. The ones that did seemed too good to be true, so I didn't bother clicking on their full profiles.

Just as I was reading about a math professor, a cup of coffee was set on my desk.

"Good morning," Aubrey whispered.

I didn't answer. I continued to scroll through online profiles; she'd get the point eventually.

She sighed. "Andrew—"

"It's *Mr. Hamilton.*" I looked up, immediately wishing that I hadn't. She looked even more stunning today than she did yesterday. She was wearing the same grey dress she'd worn to her interview, and it was tighter today than it was on that day. Her hair was falling in soft curls that fell past her shoulders, and her blue eyes were bright, hopeful.

"Can I talk to you for a second?" she asked.

"Is it about your work?"

"No..."

"Is it about *my* work?"

"No..."

"Then no. Get out."

"It's about yesterday." She stood still, making my cock stiffen as she bit her lip.

"Yesterday was a *mistake*, a regrettable moment in both of our careers, and I assure you that it won't be happening again."

"That's not what I was going to say."

"Miss Everhart," I said, standing up from my desk and walking over to her, "you and I work together professionally. If I had known the truth behind all of your ridiculous lies earlier, I would've immediately stopped talking to you. And then I would've reported you for stealing someone else's information and using it as your own. The fact that you are a *liar* remains, and unfortunately—given those circumstances and the fact that I've already fucked you, there's nothing more that needs to be said between us."

She opened her mouth to say something, but I pressed my finger against her lips.

"Nothing more," I whispered, bringing my face close to hers. "Understood?"

"You are..." Her bottom lip quivered as she jerked away from me. "You are such an *asshole*! I can't believe that I slept with you!"

"Believe it. I'm sure it'll be a very good memory for you since you hardly ever have sex."

She shook her head. "Were you pretending on the phone, too? You're nothing like the man I talked to at night, nothing like—"

"Please spare me the emotional appeal bullshit, Miss Everhart. I'll have my next cup of coffee at noon. Thanks."

"You'll be waiting." She rolled her eyes. "I'll get it when I *feel* like it."

"You're going to make me fire you over a cup of coffee?"

"To be honest, you might not want me to make your coffee, Mr. Hamilton." She narrowed her eyes at me. "There's no telling what I'll put in it."

"I fucking *dare you...*" I stepped closer.

"Is that a threat?" She shrugged.

"It's a fucking *promise*." I pushed her against the wall and pressed my lips against hers, lifting her leg around my waist.

My cock had been hard ever since she set down my coffee, and she was rubbing her hand against it through my pants right now, murmuring.

I pulled a condom out of my pocket and pressed it into her hand as I devoured her mouth—biting her soft lips, teasing her tongue with mine. If I could, I would fuck her mouth all day.

As she unzipped my pants, I slipped a hand underneath her dress and pushed her panties to the side, groaning once I felt how wet she was.

"*Andrew...*" She was taking too long with the condom, so I did it myself. The second I had it on, I slid into her deeply, biting her lips so she wouldn't scream.

I grabbed her hands and placed them around my neck. "*Always wet...*" I felt her trying to move her leg from around my waist but I held it still. "Say my name again..."

"*Yes...*" She gasped as I pounded into her, over and over and over. "*Yes...*"

"*Say it.*" I squeezed her ass.

Her murmurs were becoming louder and louder.

"My name, Aubrey..." I kissed her mouth. "Say my name..."

Her pussy was gripping my cock tighter and tighter, and her nails were clawing my neck. "I...I'm about to..."

I immediately stopped mid thrust and whispered harshly into her ear. "Say my fucking name, Aubrey..."

Her nails dug into my skin. "*Andrew...*"

At the sound of my name on her lips, I slid into her again and she came, so perfectly. I felt my own release seconds later, and could feel her burying her head in my chest to stifle her moans, but I tilted her head up.

"Stop that..."

Panting, she kept her eyes on mine. "Stop, what?"

"Hiding your voice from me..." I kissed her lips again, making no move to slide out of her, and we stood there entwined in each other for what felt like forever.

As much as I wanted to tell her to leave and get the hell out of my office, I couldn't bring myself to do it. Instead, I kissed her forehead and slowly pulled out, readjusting her dress.

After throwing away the condom, I picked up one of her heels that had fallen off and held it out for her.

Her curls were tousled all over her head, so I smoothed them back into place. As if she was returning the favor, she refastened my zipper and fixed the collar of my shirt.

Then the two of us stood staring at one another. I had no idea what the fuck just happened, and only a part of me liked it. The other half loved it.

"You need to get back to work." I tugged at the ballet slipper charm around her neck. "You still owe me that Brownstein report, demotion or not."

"You told me it wasn't a demotion."

"I took a page out of your book and *lied*." I rolled my eyes and stepped back. "Get back to work."

"Fine, *Mr. Hamilton*." She smiled and headed for the door.

"And when you come back," I added, "just leave my afternoon coffee on that bookshelf and walk out. Don't come anywhere near my desk and don't say anything to me."

"Why not?"

"Because I'll fuck you again if you do."

She blushed and stepped out of the room.

The second she was gone, I fell back into my chair and shook my head.

Twice in less than twenty four hours? Jesus...

I pulled up my latest case file, but I couldn't bring myself to read it. All I could think about was Aubrey.

I'd felt something like this before, and I knew it would lead to nothing but despair. What I felt was nothing deep, nothing all-encompassing—*yet*, but it was real, and there was nothing I could do to stop it.

I'd built the last six years of my life detaching myself from any chance of having feelings for someone else, *refusing* to build any friendships, but Aubrey had snuck by my impenetrable doors somehow. And not only had she snuck by, she'd done it with lies, something I would never allow from anyone else. Something that would make me immediately discard her and never think of her again.

I had absolutely no idea how to handle this. This was uncharted territory and I had no idea where to sail next.

Sighing, I picked up my case file and forced myself to read the first few pages so I could get a grip on myself. Before I knew it, I was lost in my work, and the only thing on my mind was how I was going to convince a jury to believe my latest client's bullshit.

Before I could call the lead prosecutor and ask what he was offering in exchange for a plea deal, I felt something hot splashing into my lap.

My goddamn coffee.

"What the hell do you think you're doing?" I dropped my papers to the desk, glaring at a red-faced Aubrey. "Did you just throw that into my lap *on purpose*?"

"I did." She nodded, and I realized there were tears in her eyes. "Bringing you your coffee is my job, right?"

"Are you fucking bipolar?"

"No, I'm just a *liar* like you said. I'm actually just like you, but at least I can admit when I haven't told you the truth, at least I have a *reason*."

"*Excuse me*?"

Tears fell down her cheeks. "You have a visitor at the front desk."

"Is it your replacement?" I asked dryly. "Because I swear to God, if these stains don't come out of my pants—"

"It's *your wife*."

end of episode one

acknowledgments

First and foremost, thank you Tamisha Draper for being the amazing and wonderful powerhouse that you are. You answer my endless phone calls (much to your husband's dismay lol), read my books over and over again, and even force me to sit down and write sex scenes when I say things like, "Would the readers really hate me if I just faded all of these sex scenes to black? No, really. Would they? They'd still love me, right?"

I don't know of anyone who would willingly work so tirelessly—anyone who would spend fifty plus hours a week working on a career that is not her own, in exchange for next to nothing…

I'm actually crying while writing this because I honestly don't deserve to have a friend as great as you. You go above and beyond with every single book I write, and you push me to make sure that each one is ten times better than the last. (If I ever make it, I swear I will find the best way to pay you back. I fucking promise.)

Thank you to all of my blogger friends that I've made so far—Bobbie Jo Malone Kirby (Why do you pick such EMOTIONAL books?! lol), Kimberly Kimball, Stephanie Locke, Lisa Pantano Kane, Michelle Kannan, and COUNTLESS more! (If I left someone out, I am sooo sorry! And hey, I self-published this, so I can easily re-upload it with your name here lol…Seriously though, I can…)

Thank you to Evelyn Guy for the final proofreading work…I noticed you didn't write much in the sex scene parts…LOL

Thank you to my mother, Lafrancine Maria, for letting me read this book to you aloud. Can't wait to see your face when I read book 2!!!

Last and NEVER EVER least, thank you to the best readers in the world! I really do love you more than you'll ever know!! (Or, as you know me to say, I. Fucking. Love. You.) So, question. How do you like Andrew? Do you think he gives Jonathan Statham a run for his money? LOL

Fucking Love You,
Whit

letter to the reader

Dear Incredible Reader,

Thank you so much for taking time out of your life to read this book! I hope you were thoroughly entertained and enjoyed reading it as much as I enjoyed writing it.

If you have any extra time, PLEASE leave a review on amazon.com, B&N.com, goodreads.com, OR send me an email (whitgracia@gmail.com) so I can personally thank you :-)

I'm forever grateful for you and your time, and I hope to be re-invited to your bookshelf with my next release.

Love,
Whitney Gracia Williams

book #2 in the reasonable doubt series

She lied to me...
She betrayed the one rule that I'm most adamant about: Honesty. Complete and utter fucking *honesty*.

I really wish she was someone else—someone who didn't have the ability to make me feel, someone I could easily discard like the hundreds of women before her.
She isn't.

I'm drawn to her like I've never been drawn to a woman before—completely captivated by the very sight of her. But unfortunately, with my past slowly re-surfacing for all of the world to see, I'll have to find a way to let her go.
She can never be mine.

COMING SOON.

more works by whitney gracia williams:

Twisted Love (*2014*)
Wasted Love (*Winter 2014*)
Reasonable Doubt #1-3 (April 2014)
My Last Resolution: A Novella (January 2014)
Mid Life Love: At Last (October 2013)
Mid-Life Love (*June 2013*)
Final Take (Jilted Bride Series)
Take Three* (Jilted Bride Series)
Take Two* (Jilted Bride Series)
Captain of My Soul: A Memoir (*July 2009*)

*These books were pulled from publication, but will be re-released in the coming months.

You can keep up with Whitney and the travels of her non-matching socks at http://www.whitneygracia.com

To be a part of the mailing list and be notified of release dates and special offers, email whitgracia@gmail.com with "Mailing List" in the subject heading.

Printed in Poland
by Amazon Fulfillment
Poland Sp. z o.o., Wrocław